I DON'T LIKE TO EAT ANTS

BY JTK BELLE

ILLUSTRATED BY
SABINE MIELKE

Picklefish
Press

Printed in the United States of America
First Printing, 2019

ISBN: 978-0-578-49951-2

JTK Belle is Jeff, Tommy, and Katie Belle.
Editor in Chief: Katie Belle
Creative Director: Tommy Belle
Illustrations by Sabine Mielke
Book Design by Michelle M White

Picklefish Press
Seattle, Washington
www.picklefishpress.com

For Emily, Connor, & James.
- JTK

To my parents. Thank you for always
letting me go my own way.
- SM

"I don't like to eat ants,"
said Anteater One.

"They don't taste very good
and **they tickle my tongue.**"

"What's wrong with you?"
said Anteater Two.

"Eating **ants** is what we do!"

"Well, not anymore," the first one said.

"I'd like some

chocolate cake instead."

4

"Chocolate cake? For goodness sake!

You'll give yourself a **tummy ache!**"

the second one **said,** as his face turned red,

and he raised his paws

and rubbed his head.

"I don't care," said Number One.

"Eating ants is just no fun.

I mean, how many ants can one anteater eat?

They're squishy. And sticky. And not very sweet."

THAT'S RIGHT!

"I just can't believe this," complained Number Two.

"Ants are **delicious!** And so good for you!"

WE'RE VERY SQUISHY!

"You eat them, then," said Anteater One.

"I'm going to eat this cinnamon bun.

And if I'm still hungry," he said with a smile,

"I'll nibble this grilled cheese sandwich awhile."

IS THAT TRUE, ABOUT THE TEETH?

8

The second one stared in disbelief.

"You know that anteaters don't have teeth. So how do you think you're going to chew a cinnamon bun?" said Anteater Two.

I DON'T KNOW,
AND I DON'T CARE TO FIND OUT.

Number One replied,

"There's nothing to it.

I'll cut it into bits and chew it.

Or I'll make a nice salad from flowers and plants.

Something, **anything**, other than **ants!**"

The second one huffed
and turned his head.

He pointed to his snout
and said,

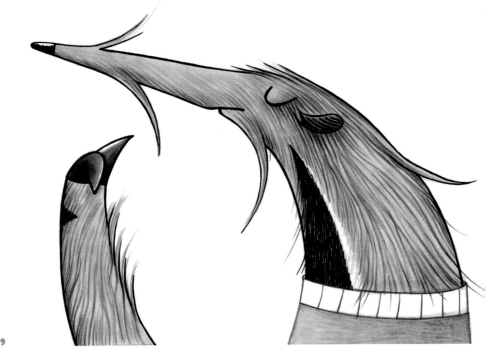

"Why is it, then,
do you suppose,

an anteater has such a
very long nose?"

"For sniffing all the pretty flowers?

And separating sweets from sours?"

"**No!** For burrowing down into hard-to-reach spaces, and finding **ants** in their hiding places!"

UH-OH.

RUN!

"**Bah!** No more ants for me, my friend.
My ant-eating days have come to an end.

I won't, I shan't, **I simply can't . . .**
eat even so much as **one more** little ant."

"Why then . . . you won't be an ant-eater at all.
You'll be a Chocolate-Cake-Eater!
A Cinnamon-Bun-Eater!
A Grilled-Cheese-and-Salad-
You-Made-From-
a-Plant-Eater!"

"What's in a name?" said Anteater One.

"Let's try some new things! Let's go have some fun!

I happen to know a good restaurant.

I'll buy you some lunch — whatever you want."

THEY'RE LEAVING!

PHEW!

"*I* want ants."

And so off they went to Anteater Three's,

where they sat at a table, enjoying the breeze.

"I'll have the **peanut butter and jelly**,"

said Anteater One as he rubbed his belly.

"Just a **bowl** of **ants** for me,"

said Anteater Two to Anteater Three.

"I'm sorry, but we're all out of ants today.

Can I interest you in a **PB&J?**"

"Ugh! Peanut butter and jelly?

Why did you make me come to this deli?

I'm an **anteater!**

That's **all** I eat, don't you see?

No **peanut butter and jelly** for me!"

"Oh, come now, my friend. Give it a **chance**.

There's more to fine dining than just eating **ants**."

Anteater Three's
Peanut Butter & Jelly Deli

"**OK**, I give up! Enough already!

Bring me a peanut butter and jelly!

I'll take **one tiny bite** of the sandwich, alright?

But I'm already losing my appetite."

Home of the World's Best
Peanut Butter & Jelly Sandwich

Anteater One took a sip of his drink,
and said to his friend,

"Well, what do you think?"

"Hmmmmm . . . Mmmmmmm . . . Yum, **yum, yum!**"

said Anteater Two as he ate the last crumb.

OOH, STRAWBERRY!

HE LIKES IT!

Home of the World's Best
Peanut Butter & Jelly Sandwich

"Well, my friend, now what do you say?
Would you like **another** PB&J?"

said Number One with a wink and a grin,
as he licked peanut butter from under his chin.

"**Yes! Yes!** Another one please!"

said Anteater Two to Anteater Three.

Home of the World's Best
Peanut Butter & Jelly Sandwich

WE SHOULD COME HERE MORE OFTEN.

I LIKE THIS PLACE.

"I could eat two, **or three,**
or even **four** more!

Why didn't you tell me about
this before?"

"I think I might have mentioned it to you,"
said Anteater One to Anteater Two.

"But I'm glad you tried something other than ants.

You never know what you'll like,
'til you give it a chance."

28

"Yes, you're right," **Number Two replied.**

"But it would be even better with **ants** on the side."

TIME TO GET OUT OF HERE...

THE END!

JTK Belle

is Jeff, Tommy, and Katie Belle.
They live in Seattle, Washington.
Visit www.picklefishpress.com to find more of
their books and see what they're up to next.

Sabine Mielke (Juniemond)

lives with her three sighthounds in Berlin.
She loves creating, scribbling, drawing and painting
by night with coffee and chocolate.